THE SCHOOL CAT

AND THE ZOMBIE SKELETON

BY
THE THIRD GRADE
OF CITY NEIGHBORS HAMILTON

City Neighbors Zombie Press

Baltimore, MD

City Neighbors Zombie Press
5609 Sefton Avenue
Baltimore, MD 21214
www.cityneighborshamilton.org

Cover art by Ben, Gabe, and Jeremy.

Cover design by Caleb.

The Magic School Cat and the Zombie Skeleton / City Neighbors Hamilton Third Grade Class and Ms. Marilyn. — 1st Ed.
ISBN 978-0-9963237-3-4

Contents

Dedication

This book is dedicated to Principal Obi Okobi.

Thank you for leadership and always encouraging us to do our most excellent work.

CHAPTER 1

NO LONGER A NORMAL SCHOOL DAY

Our class really has good luck. This year we got Ms. Chelsea, the greatest teacher in the school. We don't mind her fashion or her style. It's her personality that really gets us. Usually Ms. Chelsea comes in looking like a fashionista — you see, she really loves fashion. However, today Ms. Chelsea came in not looking so good. She was limping and had a big, bloody gash on her head.

As she took her seat, the kids hurried to the white, skull-shaped carpet. Brittany ran up to Ms. Chelsea and asked, "Are you OK?"

Ms. Chelsea replied, "No ... It's been a rough morning, and I need your help. We need to get to the Zombie Graveyard and to get there we need to take Nyan the School Cat."

"Why are we going to the Zombie graveyard?" shouted Diamond.

"The Zombie graveyard is ssssss-spooky and dangerous," hissed Stewie the snake.

We all knew that Zombie Graveyard was the one place in town nobody goes to. "I can tell you more as we ride Nyan Cat, but right now we need to get going," explained Ms. Chelsea.

CHAPTER 2

THE ZOMBIE GRAVEYARD

Quickly we all crawled up onto Nyan Cat. "We are going to the Zombie Graveyard because we must collect The King Zombie's bones," explained Ms. Chelsea. We flew on Nyan Cat with Ms. Chelsea and landed in the spooky graveyard.

"The reason why we have to collect The King Zombie's bones is because then all the zombies in the world will turn back into humans," said Ms. Chelsea. We all gasped when we saw The Zombie Graveyard.

"Ahhhh! Zombies!" screamed Diamond A. Stewie hid behind a gravestone, and then he slithered out and scared Brittany.

Stewie, Brittany, and Diamond B. got on Nyan Cat. They decided to search separately in The Zombie Graveyard to look for the ribs, clavicle, and sternum. Brittany was scared of zombies, so she went to look with Diamond. When Stewie looked for the bones by himself, he could see something in the tree. He

used his strong muscles and his scales to go up the big tree.

There in the tree, a zombie was guarding the sternum. Surprisingly, the zombie was scared of snakes and ran away. Stewie said, “That was easy.” Stewie took the sternum, put it under his watch, and slithered away.

Meanwhile Diamond B. and Brittany went back to Nyan Cat. They got into special suits because there was a virus underground where they needed to go to get the bones. They went underground and started looking for the bones (specifically the ribs and collarbone).

While they were underground, a zombie suddenly came up to Nyan Cat. Unsure of what to do, he farted a huge fart that smelled like cupcakes and sweetness.

"That was really weird," Nyan said to himself.

Then the zombie smelled it and ran away because he didn't like the smell of colorful sweetness since he was such a dark person.

The girls were still looking for their bones, so Stewie went underground with them. As soon as Stewie arrived, Brittany shouted, "I found the clavicle\collar bone!"

While searching for the rib cage, a zombie popped out of nowhere and followed them.

"Ahhh!" squealed Brittany. But standing up to her fear, tall and proud, she used her karate moves to defend herself and her friends. She kicked her leg up as high as she could and shouted "hiya" as the zombie head rolled to the ground. Then suddenly, the rib cage fell out of the bag that the zombie was trying to hide from them.

Diamond screamed, "The rib cage! The zombie had it the whole time."

They climbed out of the underground as soon as possible and got on Nyan Cat.

CHAPTER 3

THE KING ZOMBIE

When Brittany, Diamond, and Stewie got back safely on Nyan Cat, we got off Nyan Cat and went on our search. "OK, now all we need to do is find is the patella, femur, tibia, and fibula," Lola B. said.

"O-OK!" Milan said.

"Yo! Are you scared?" Timmy Turner said.

"Y-yeah, I am," Milan said.

"Come on guys!" Lola B. said. "We can do this." So we went on our search for the bones.

"Look guys! I found a patella and the other bones!" Lola said. Lola ran to get the bones. When she grabbed them, a zombie came out from the ground. "AAAAAHHH ... A ZOMBIE!" Lola screamed. Lola ran away from Timmy Turner and Milan.

"OK, now that was weird." Timmy Turner said.

"Well, she does hate zombies," Milan said.

Meanwhile, Lola was running in a dark and scary place, where all the zombies were looking for her.

She hid behind a black tree. "OMG... I hate zombies so bad," Lola said. "Y-you're The King Zombie," said a scared Lola.

"Yes I am, and you will pay! MINIONS!" shouted The King Zombie.

Suddenly, zombies came out of the ground. "RUN!!!" said Milan.

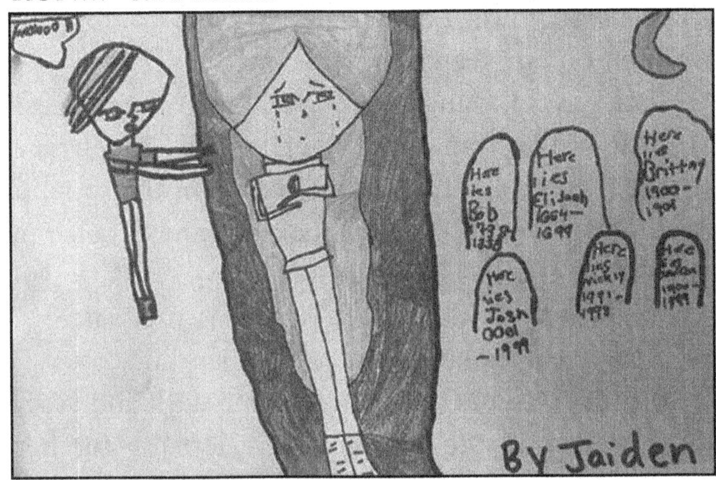

"Brrrrrrrains!" the zombie said.

Lola was so scared. "Oh no!" Lola said. "I know I'm a Devil and all, but I am scared of zombies." She turned into a Devil to fly into the tree she was hiding behind.

'Brrrrrrrrrrrrains!" the zombie said in the tree.

"Flash!" Timmy Turner said showing his shiny gold chain to the Zombie.

"Ahhhhhh!" said the zombie as he ran away.

As quick as they could, Milan, Timmy Turner, and Lola rushed back with the bones to get on Nyan Cat.

CHAPTER 4

THE SEARCH FOR THE MISSING SPINE AND THE SHOULDER BLADES

"Lola, can you find the lower back and the upper back?" asked Jordan.

"Yes," said Lola.

"OK, thanks," said Jordan. "I will look for the neck, sacrum, and coccyx."

"Can I help?" said Lola.

"Not yet. I am sorry," said Jordan.

"OK, fine... but can I find the neck?" said Lola.

"OK," said Jordan.

"OK, let's get off Nyan Cat and go find these bones! Devil and DJ have to look for 23 vertebrae," said Lola.

"Hey, just find what you can, OK?!" said Devil.

"AHHH!" shouted Lola.

"I hear Lola screaming" said DJ.

"Me, too!" said Devil.

"OK, let's get started," said DJ, and they all set off in search of bones.

When they found their bones, DJ said, "OK, let's go back to Nyan Cat."

Devil, DJ, Jordan, and Lola went back to Nyan the School Cat. "I have 13 vertebrae. How many do you have?" said Devil.

"Ten!" said DJ.

"I see a zombie on the back of Nyan Cat! We need to push the zombie off of Nyan the School Cat," Devil said.

When they pushed the Zombie off of Nyan Cat, they were all safe again with the bones they needed to complete the mission.

CHAPTER 5

SKULL OF THE DEAD

We got off Nyan cat and walked around. "I see something over there," said Smashberg.

"What is it?" said Dabbing Flash.

"I think it's a skull," said Blob.

"Remember, we have to get the jaw, too," Blob said to Smashberg.

"Yes, yes, yes ... "

We walked over to it. "Oh, it's nothing. Just some sticks," said Dabbing Flash. Squash, squash.

"Oh god! I stepped in rotting zombie flesh!" said Smashberg.

"Ha! Look at that metal vase over there," said Blob.

"It's on a grave," said Smashberg.

"Waaaaa!" shouted Dabbing Flash.

We walked over to it. "Ha, Smashberg. I dare you to pull it," said Dabbing Flash.

"Why?" said Smashberg.

"I don't know. Something could happen," said Dabbing Flash.

"OK," said Smashberg.

Smashberg pulled the vase. "Well, something is happening," said Blob as the grave opened to a tomb.

When Smashberg pulled the vase, the zombies rushed out. Smashberg, Dabbing Flash, and Blob got

Smashberg's hammer to smash all of the zombies' heads. Blob charged in to attack and kill the zombies. As we were getting out of the tomb, we noticed that we left Blob.

"I'm in the tomb!" shouted Blob. Smashberg picked Blob up and carried him back to Nyan cat. They couldn't leave their friend behind. We hopped on Nyan cat and back to school we went.

CHAPTER 6

THE IMPORTANT HUMERUS, RADIUS, AND ULNA

When we got off Nyan Cat, we had to find the ulna, radius, and humerus. "I am surprised we have to find the radius and humerus. I'm surprised we have to find all these bones," said Rosey. They looked in the dark part of the graveyard. "I'm so scared," said Paige.

"I think I see something," said Diamond A.

When we were looking for all the bones, Xernez climbed the tree and found the ulna.

"Paige!" Rosy yelled. "I found the radius!"

"Where?" Xernez yelled.

"It's on the grave!" Rosey replied.

"I am on it," Diamond A. said smoothly not knowing what awaited her.

"So we need to find th—" Paige said not finishing her sentence.

"AHHH!" Diamond A. yelled.

"Let's go," Paige said. We looked at the grave yard.

"OMG!" Rosey said not so good.

"That's our friend," Paige replied.

Xernez grabbed the lever and the floor dropped. We were not surprised. We saw Diamond. But unlike us, we suspected she was actually not scared. She looked a little proud. She quickly jumped around. "Oh you guys," she said gladly. "It's just us! Let's go."

Xernez said, "Yeah."

"This place gives me the chills," Rosey said.

"No. She meant let's go find our bones," said Diamond A.

Just then, we went up from the ground, and we found the radius bone underneath the gravestone. The humerus was really hard to find. We looked all over the place. Just then, Paige had a flashback of ZOMBIES.

"Zombies!" she yelled, and zombies came from all corners — north, east, south, west. Xernez turned into an owl (she is very secretive and magical) and flew in the air.

"That zombie!" Rosie yelled (the wind was blowing so hard it made us so quiet that we couldn't hear unless we yelled). There was a zombie with our bone.

We went onto the ground. "Remember, zombies are afraid of cats," Paige reminded us.

"Oh yeah," Xernez whispered and then talked in cat form. "Meow," she said, and all the zombies were gone except the one we wanted — the one with the humerus. Finally, we got our bone, but we had to find each other. Diamond A. was with Xernez, Paige was in a tree, and Rosey was beneath a gravestone.

After we found the humerus, radius, and ulna, Diamond wandered into the other part of the graveyard. Rosey followed. Diamond A. was in the darkest part of the graveyard. Rosey was so scared she was holding on very tight.

"Dang! you must be scared," Diamond said. They called the rest of the group over and then pressed their watches. The group joined and went back on Nyan Cat.

When we got on Nyan the School Cat, Diamond A. told Ms. Chelsea how we found the humerus, radius, and the ulna. The ulna was in the tree, the radius was under the gravestone, and the humerus was with the zombie. Ms. Chelsea told the class what we told her. We were excited and so was everyone else.

"OMG!" said Paige. "We found the humerus, radius, and ulna!" It was so fun finding the humerus, radius, and ulna.

CHAPTER 7

THE DANCING PHALANGES

As soon as Bella and Jessie had the chance, they immediately went to find their bones. Bella started digging near a graveyard. While Bella was digging, she heard Jessie scream, "AHHH! Help! It's a zombie! Help!"

"Hold on," she said. As Bella was running to Jessie to help her, she tripped over something and said, "Bella, Bella, what is it?"

"Ah!" screamed both Bella and Jessie.

Bella and Jessie saw a zombie. They both screamed so loud that the zombie's head fell off. They ran away to Ms. Chelsea. Ms. Chelsea grabbed them to put them back on Nyan School Cat. They both took deep breaths, trying not to think about what just happened. They sat down on the Nyan Cat's bus seats. They both looked out Nyan Cat's widows. They both saw the zombies looking around for them.

Bella said, "Get down!"

Jessie followed her instructions, and they both crouched down.

Jessie said, “Shhh ...” and Bella put her hands over her mouth.

Bella whispered, “Don't move.”

Jessie gripped Nyan Cat's seats. Jessie said, “I think he's gone.”

Bella and Jessie argued about who was going to open the door.

"You do it," Jessie said.

"Well, I don't wanna get killed," Bella said.

"Ugh. Fine. I'll check."

Jessie looked up and slowly started to stand to look out the window.

"OH MY GOSH! There are more!"

"What?" Bella said. "Where is Ms. Chelsea?"

Then they both turned and looked at each other. "We need to go back out and find Ms. Chelsea!" Bella said.

"Are you crazy? We can get eaten!" Jessie said.

"I don't know about you, but I'm going."

"Fine. Just make this quick," Jessie said.

They opened the door and they tiptoed. They made their way to Ms. Chelsea and tapped her on her shoulder. "Pssst. Ms. Chelsea ... be careful—"

"Girls, I'm so glad to see you, too!"

"Shhh," they said.

"Why?" said Ms. Chelsea.

"No time to explain. We need to go."

"I feel something on the ground. Look! It's a whole foot bone — two of them! Hurry. Let's grab them to connect them to the skeleton!"

CHAPTER 8

THE EXPLORING OF THE MISSING PHALANGES

Ed and Snivy got off Nyan Cat. They were walking through the graveyard. "The graveyard looks empty," said Snivy. "When are we go—"

Thump!

"What was that?" said Ed.

"It looks like a hatch," said Snivy. They opened the hatch to the underground layer.

Bang!

"What the?!" said Snivy.

"Z-Z-ZOMBIES," said Ed.

"Look. I think we found a hand!" said Snivy.

"RUUUUUN!" said Ed.

They climbed up as fast as they could and started to run with the hand. "We can take them ..." said Ed. "Well, they're zombies. They're easy to take down."

Slap!

Snivy smacked a zombie with the hand.

Bang!

Ed punched a zombie in the head.

Slice!

Snivy sliced a zombie with his claws. There was still at least 9,000 zombies left to take down.

"I don't think we can do this," said Ed.

"There is no problem here," said Snivy. "I have a laser eye, claws, and some robot replacements."

"Are you sure?" said Ed.

"Yep," said Snivy.

As they were running, Snivy elbowed 11 zombies. "OWWW! I GOT BIT!!"

"OH NO! Keep running," said Ed.

"BUT IT HURTS!!" screamed Snivy.

"WE WILL BE DEAD IF WE DON'T!" said Ed.

They ran even faster and faster and faster until they ran out of breath. "Are they gone yet?" said Snivy.

"Uh-huh," said Ed.

When Snivy looked at the bite, there was a big bloody smear on his arm. "Can you wrap my arm up?" said Snivy.

"Sure," said Ed.

As Ed wrapped Snivy's arm, the blood faded through the cloth. "How are we going to get back to Nyan Cat?" said Snivy.

"After we find the other hand, then we'll discuss it," explained Ed.

"We should go now so we can find the hand," said Snivy.

"You're right," said Ed.

Snivy and Ed were walking by and saw a bunch of zombies guarding the last hand. "There it is!" whispered Ed.

"Shhhhhh! You're going to ruin the whole plan!" said Snivy. "And I have this all planned out."

"I will get under the leaves," said Ed. "You distract him Snivy."

As Ed sneaked over, Snivy was distracting the zombies.

"Nah-Nah-Nah-Boo-Boo!" shouted Snivy.

All the zombies looked at Snivy. Snivy beamed the zombies, and Ed jumped out with the hand.

"Nice!" said Ed.

"Let's go back to Nyan Cat," said Snivy, and they walked back to Nyan Cat.

CHAPTER 9

DUNGEON OF THE DEAD

We started walking into the darkest and scariest part of the graveyard.

"Ahhh, this is dark!" said Techy. We passed a lot of graves, but none of them said anything about the pelvis or femur.

"Here, over here!" cried Johnny. He had found a grave that said that The Skelly Bones (The King Zombie's) pelvis and femur imploded. But it had tree roots all over it.

So Johnny said, "What are we going to do?" Johnny is very strong because he is a mega Cat and he is fat because he eats a lot. So Johnny suggested that he could push it down, but Bob magically summoned an axe because Bob is magical and knowledgeable. He chopped through the tree roots.

Together we pushed the grave over, and a secret stairwell appeared. We started walking down the stairwell but found it was too dark.

"I'll summon a torch," said Bob.

"Good thinking," said Johnny. We continued. When we got to the bottom, we realized we were in a dungeon.

"Cool," said Techy.

"NO! Not cool," said Johnny.

"Let's take a look around," said Bob, ignoring Johnny.

"Oh look! I think I found the bones," said Techy.

"WAIT!" said Bob. "We don't know if there are any booby-traps!"

"Good point," said Johnny.

We looked around for a little while but found nothing out of the ordinary.

"I think it's safe," said Bob.

"Then let's go," said Johnny.

We grabbed the bones that were chained to the wall. We pulled and pulled, and suddenly, the wall gave way! It fell to the ground with a sickening crack. When the dust cleared, a musty passageway appeared. "Let's go in," said Techy.

We went in and looked around the room. Johnny saw a glowing pelvis in a corner of the room. Bob saw a femur in another corner, and Techy saw the other femur. Then a ladder fell down, and we started climbing out.

When we got off the ladder, we found we were in a tree. Techy said, “Um ... where are we?”

“I think we’re in a tree,” said Bob sarcastically.

We looked down and saw a hoard of zombies under us. We jumped down

"Ahhh!" said Techy.

“That’s a lot of zombies,” replied Johnny.

“Let’s destroy them,” said Bob.

They jumped down, and while they were fighting, Bob told a joke. “Why didn’t the skeleton cross the graveyard?”

“I don’t know,” said Techy.

“Because he didn’t have the guts to,” explained Bob.

PEW PEW was the sound of Bob shooting plasma. After they destroyed all 375 zombies, Johnny said, “We probably destroyed two-thirds of the graveyard.”

Then we walked to Nyan the School Cat and helped the class fight zombies.

CHAPTER 10

THE FINAL BATTLE

Finally, the entire class had gathered the bones they needed and had made it back to Nyan Cat. We all jumped off Nyan School Cat and prepared for battle. We pulled out anything we could fight the zombies with, but we didn't see any zombies. We also pulled out The King Zombie's bones, so we could reconstruct his skeleton and fully banish all zombies in the world.

Suddenly, we heard The King Zombie say, "Rise my minions!" Hundreds of thousands of millions of zombies rised from the ground, so we ...

CHARGED!

In less than a minute, The King Zombie was 243 feet tall, and he picked up a building as tall as the Empire State Building and crumbled it into a sword. He swung the sword and hit a plane, which fell on Johnny.

"Oh no!" cried the class. But then Johnny got up and threw the sword at The King Zombie! It hit him in the nose. A gushing of blood, the size of Niagara Falls, started flowing when his nose fell off!

"Oh, that's bad," said Smashberg.

While The King Zombie was distracted by the gushing of blood, the class quickly reconstructed the skeleton of The King Zombie. They were very careful to place the bones exactly in the correct place. Everything they had learned in class with Ms. Chelsea came in handy as they swiftly worked to reconstruct the skeleton like a puzzle.

When the last phalange bone was secured, the gushing blood stopped, and The King Zombie's ghost melted away. All the Zombies in the world had disappeared.

Once again, Ms. Chelsea's class had saved the day!

PART 2

THE REPORTS

SOMETHING SOMETHING STERNUM BY STEWIE GRIFFIN (AIDAN)

Did you know that your chest moves in and out and that makes it so much easier to take in bigger breaths? The sternum or breastbone connects to twelve pairs of ribs. There are four ribs not attached to the sternum, but they are attached to the spine. Your rib cage protects your heart, lungs, spleen, and liver. It was fun researching the rib cage.

Sources:
www.kidsfacts.com

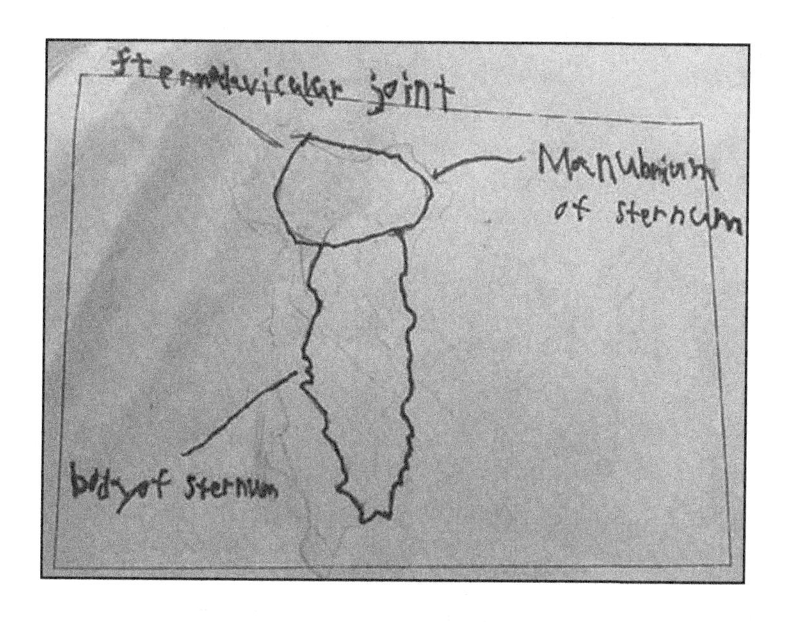
joint
Manubrium
of sternum
sternum

THE SKULL OF THE DEAD

BY ALLEN

The brain is protected by several bones, and also 22 bones make a skull. The skull is connected to the jaw. In your brain are three layers of tissue called the meninges. The skull also includes cartilage. The upper bone is called the mandible, the lower bone is called the maxilla. The skull protects the eyes, ears, and tongue. Your skull is connected to the jaw. Your 3 pound (1.4 kilogram) brain needs a home — your skull.

The Skull of The Dead
skull
Jaw
Makiell

AMAZING RIBS
BY AMAIYA

Your ribs are one of the most important bones. They protect your soft organs like your heart and lungs. Your floating ribs are the ones at the bottom that don't connect with your sternum, and you can call it clavicle. Did you know out of 20 people only 1 person has an extra pair of ribs? Now isn't that cool? When you breathe, your rib cage goes up and down, and you also get rid of used air!

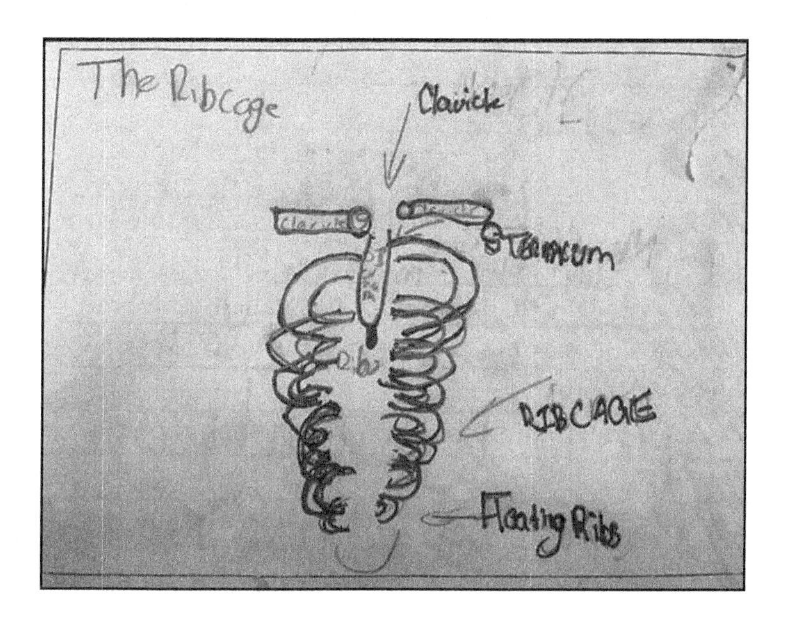
The Ribcage
Clavicle
RIBCAGE
Floating Ribs

STRONG AND FLEXIBLE BY JORDAN (AMINAH)

Did you know that the spine is a flexible bone?
The spine is the shape of the letter S.
It is made up of bones called vertebrae.

Your upper spine has 12 vertebrae your lower spine has 5 vertebrae.

Also, your spine and your skull lock together at the neck.

The total number of vertebrae in the spine is 33. I had fun learning about the spine!

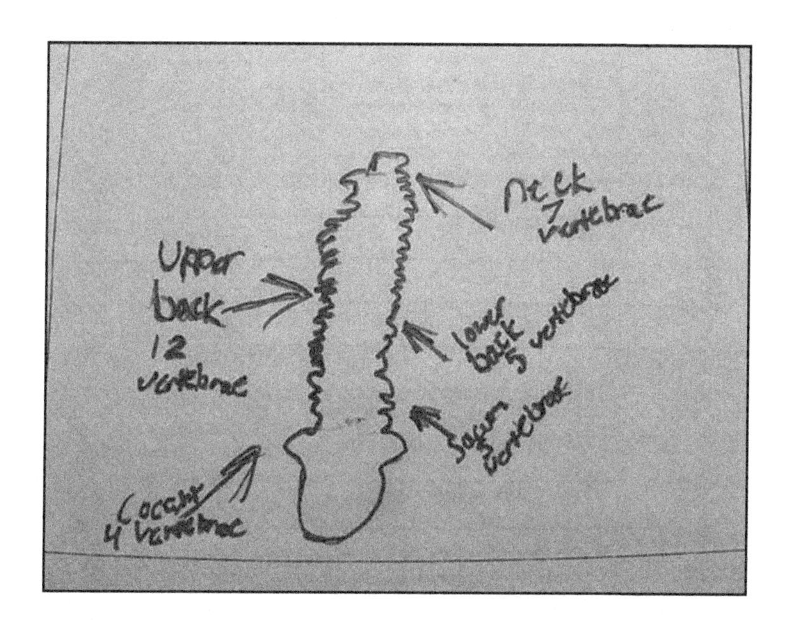
neck
7
vertebrae
Upper
back
12
vertebrae
lower
back
5 vertebrae
5
vertebrae
4 vertebrae

THE LONG SPINE
BY DEVIL (ANDRE)

The spine is called your backbone. Vertebrae are the tiny bones in your spine. The spine has 33 vertebrae. The sacrum is 5 vertebrae often fused together into one bone. The spine is a column of hollow bones called vertebrae. Your spine is locked into your skull, and also, the spine is locked into the pelvis. Love Devil.

Source:

The Search for the Missing Bones the Magic School Bus

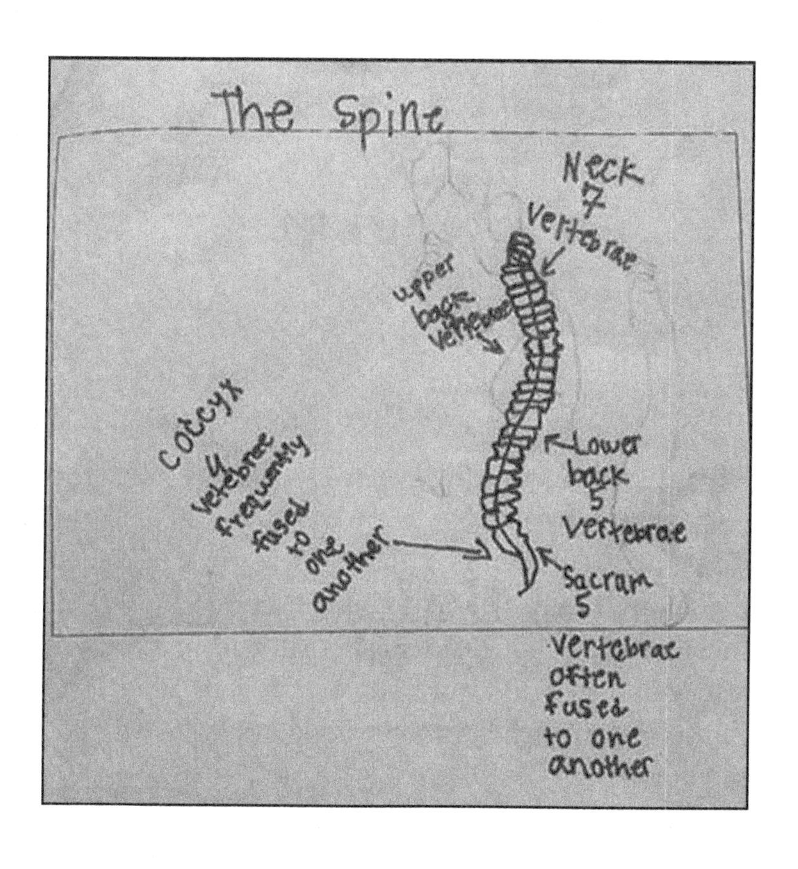
The Spine
Neck
7
Vertebrae
upper
back
vertebrae
Coccyx
4
vertebrae
frequently
fused
to
one
another
Lower
back
5
Vertebrae
Sacrum
5
vertebrae
often
fused
to one
another

THE IMPORTANT HUMERUS BY DIAMOND A. (AUTUMN)

Did you know the upper arm bone is called the humerus?

Also sometimes, the humerus can be called the funny bone. The adult humerus develops from the individual bones in the fetus. The humerus is also connected to your radius and your ulna. The funny bone is actually not a bone at all. It is a spot in your elbow.

The humerus is classified structurally as a long bone because the humerus is wide. Did you know the humerus fits into a ball and socket joint? The socket is called glenoid cavity. There is a lot to learn about the humerus.

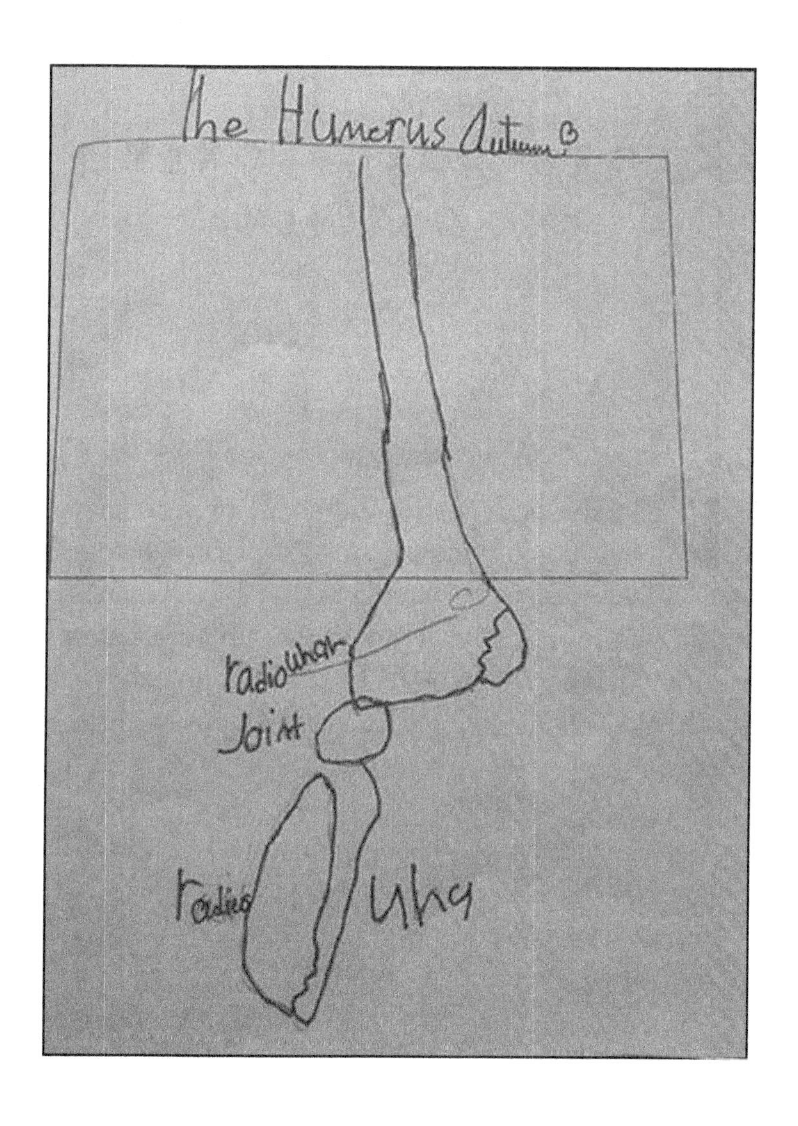
The Humerus
radiounar
Joint
radio
Una

LONG LONG BONES
BY BOB (BEN)

Did you know, the femur is the largest bone in the body? Also, the shape of your pelvis helps your femurs stay in place. Don't forget, your femur is 20 inches by the time you're an adult. By the way, your femur makes up for a quarter of your height. Lastly, your femur is about 2 inches wide. As a result, my group learned a lot about the femur.

Sources:
You're Tall in The Morning and Short in The Night
Muscles and Bones
Magic School Bus

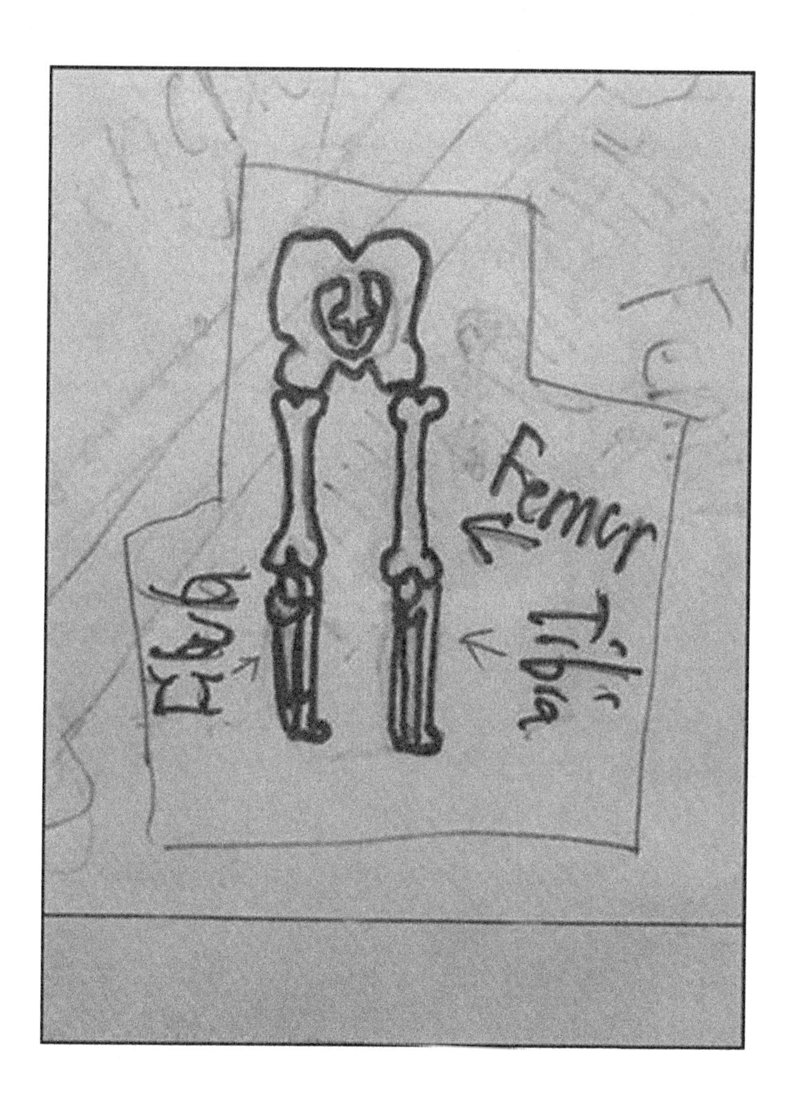
Femur
Tibia

IT'S SO JAWSOME
BY SMASHBERG (CALEB)

The strongest and biggest bone in the face is the mandible. The lower jaw is called the mandible, and the upper jaw is called the maxilla. Also, the name mandible comes from Latin. Your teeth sit on your mandible and maxilla like they're watching TV. There is a lot to learn about the jawsome mandible.

Sources:

www.scienekidz.co.mz human

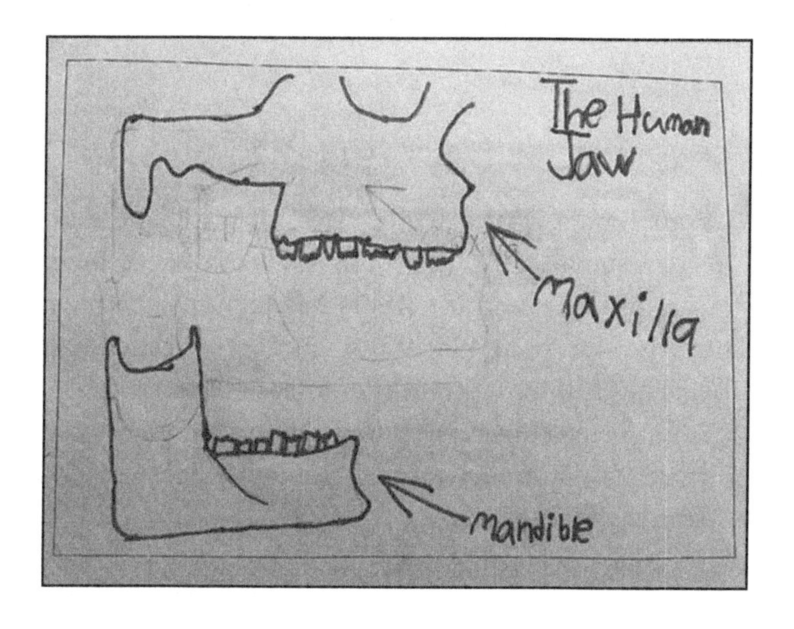
The Human Jaw
Maxilla
mandible

THE 2 CRAZY BONES BY TIMMY TURNER (ELI)

Your Fibula is next to the tibia, so if look at your leg you will see a fat spot. Below your knee, there are 2 bones, and the fibula has teeny tiny bones. The large shin bone in front of your legs is called the tibia. The thinner bone to the outside is the fibula.

Your skeleton has 206 bones when you are a teen, and you have 300 bones when you are a baby.

Source:
The Magic School Bus

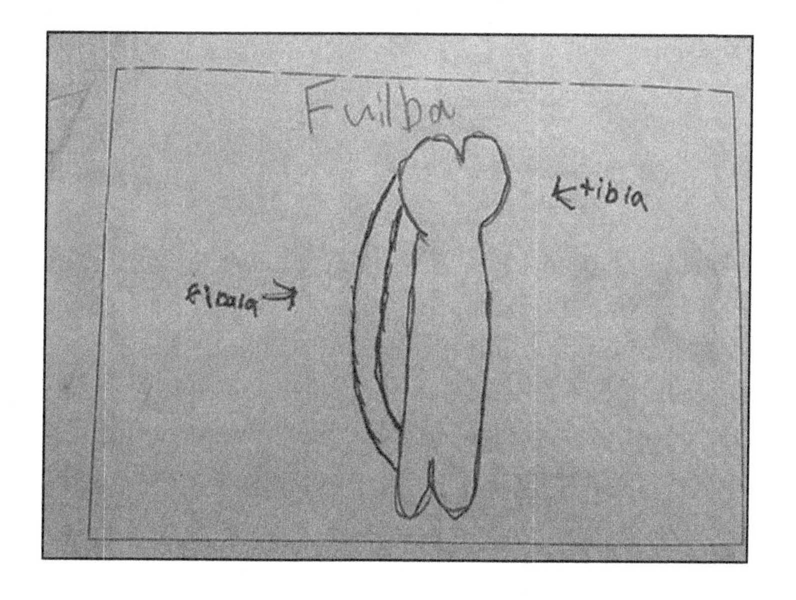
Fuilba
<tibia
Fibula→

54 CRAZY BONES BY THE DEAD HAND (ELIJAH)

Did you know that your phalanges are your fingers? Also, there are exactly 27 bones in a human hand. Both of your hands has 29 major joints. Most people in the world are right handed, and most of us aren't left handed. However, a fun fact is that your fingers are designed to work with your thumb.

It was fun writing about the phalanges.

Source:

Human Body Delta Education

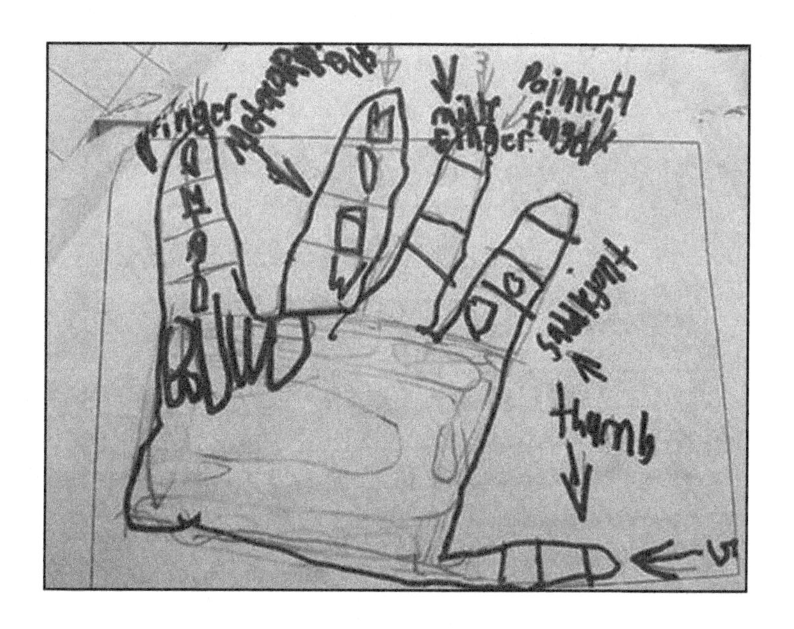
finger
Pointer4
thumb

THE AWESOME CLAVICLE
BY BRITTANY (FAYLISE)

The collarbone is the part of your shoulder girdle. The collarbone is also called the clavicle. Your clavicle holds your arm in place. The clavicle is between the scapula and sternum. The clavicle is a very important bone for the ribs and the humerus.

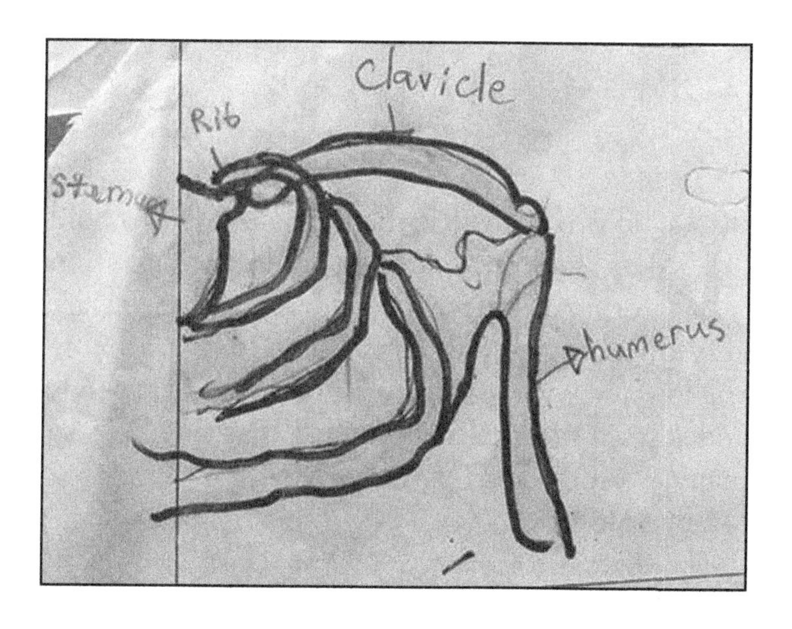
Clavicle
Rib
humerus

THE COOL PELVIS
BY JOHNNY (GABE)

Did you know that the pelvis is used to hold up the reproduction and the digestion organs? The male and female pelvis are very different because the female pelvis is more shallow and wide. Also, the plural of pelvis is pelvis, and it's symmetrical. I'm so glad that there are so many awesome facts on the pelvis!

Sources:
www.KidzSearch.com

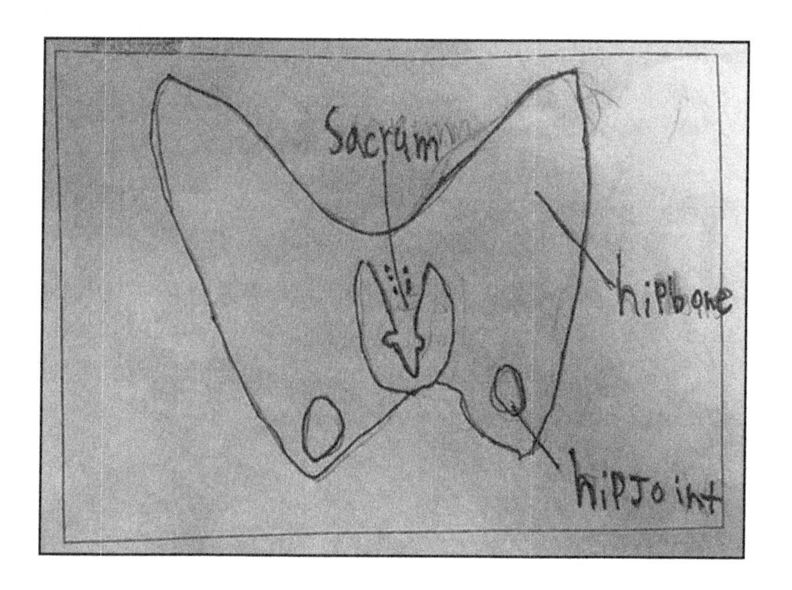
Sacrum
hipbone
hipJoint

THE LONGEST BONE!
BY LOLA (JAIDEN)

Did you know that the tibia is on one side and the fibula is on the other?

Also, did you know the femur is the thigh bone?

The tibia and fibula can help you walk, run, and skip and bend in many ways.

The shin that is the tibia is connected to the femur, patella, and fibula.

WOW! The human body is super cool to learn about!

Sources:

Muscles and Bones by James Saunderson

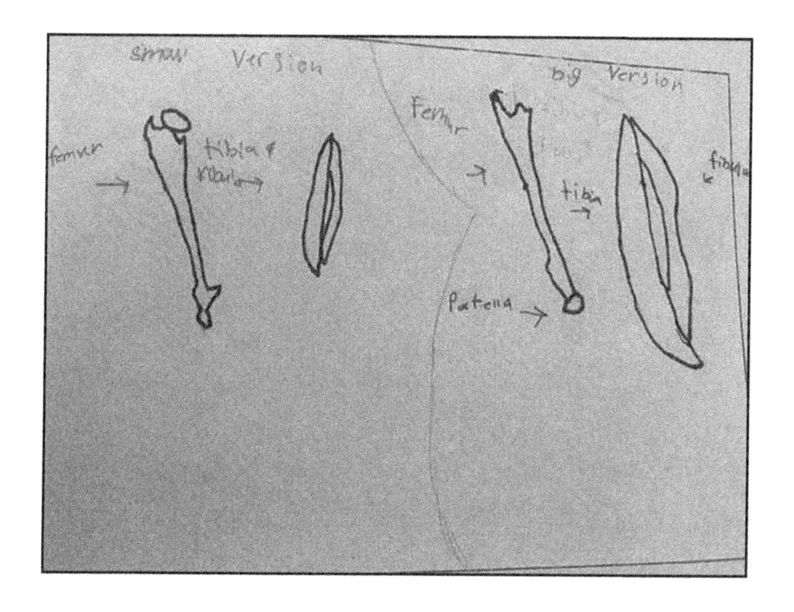
Version
tibia &
big Version
tibia
Patella

BENDY FINGERS
BY SNIVY (JEREMY)

Did you know that your fingers are designed to work with your thumb? The thumb is the only place the saddle joint is found in the hand or possibly the human body. The saddle joint allows the thumb to go forward, backward, and side -to-side. The saddle joint is at the bottom of your thumb. Your wrist is called the carpal bones. These facts have helped me learn a lot about the phalanges.

Source:
Human Body by Delta Education

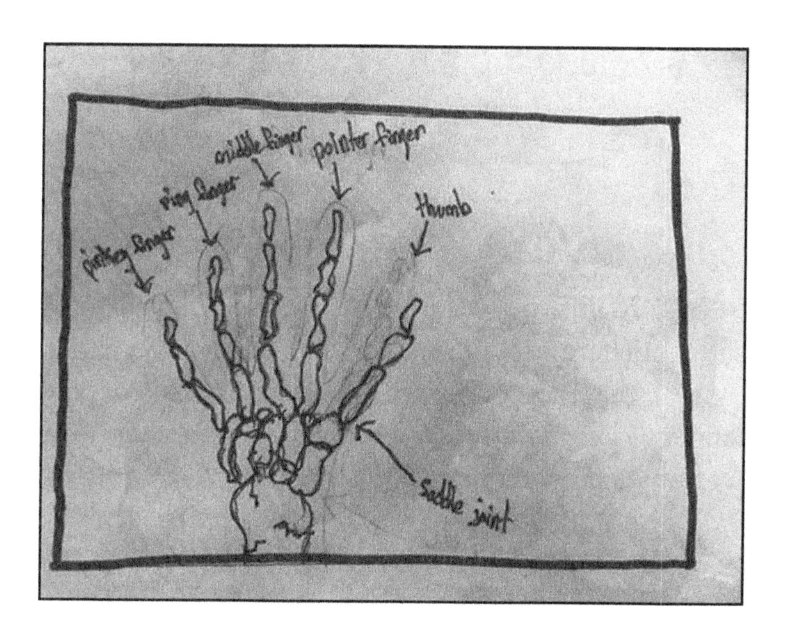
pinky finger
ring finger
middle finger
pointer finger
thumb
saddle joint

THE CASE FOR THE DANCING PHALANGES

BY JOSLEN KLENNERT

Did you know there are 26 bones in your feet? There are 3 bones in the toe. The bones in the toe connected together are called phalanges. The phalanges are called metacarpals. The feet holds the weight of your body.

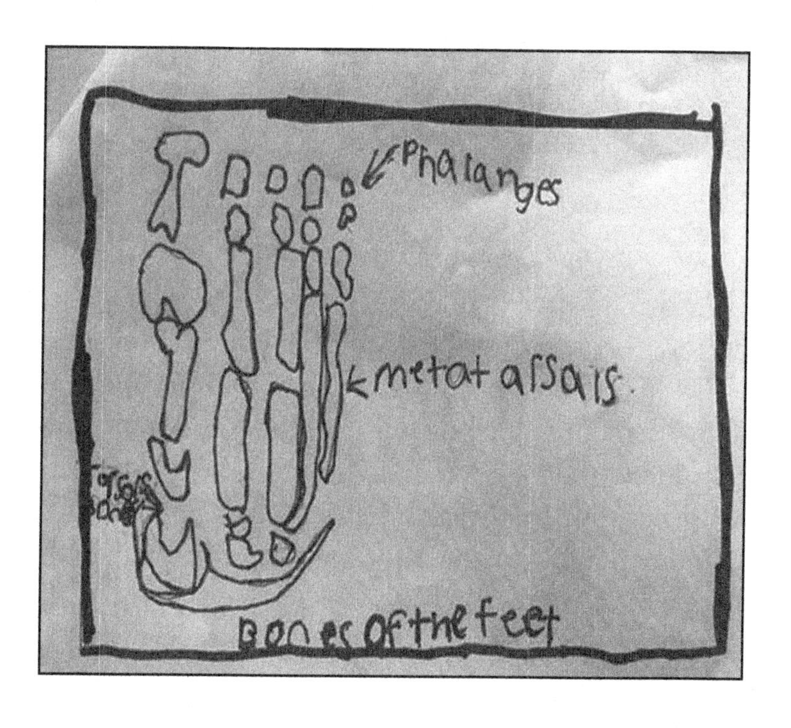
Phalanges
metatarsals
Bones of the feet

LONG, LONGER, LONGEST! BY TECHY (JULIAN)

Did you know the adult femur is about 20 inches long?! Next, the femur is about 2 inches thick at full size. Also, I don't think you know that the femur is hollow as well as filled with marrow. Lastly, your femur makes up a quarter of your height. In the end, my group learned a lot about the femur.

Sources:

Tall in the Morning but Shorter at Night by Melvin and Gilda Berger

Them Bones by Ian Dicks

The Magic School Bus by Eva More

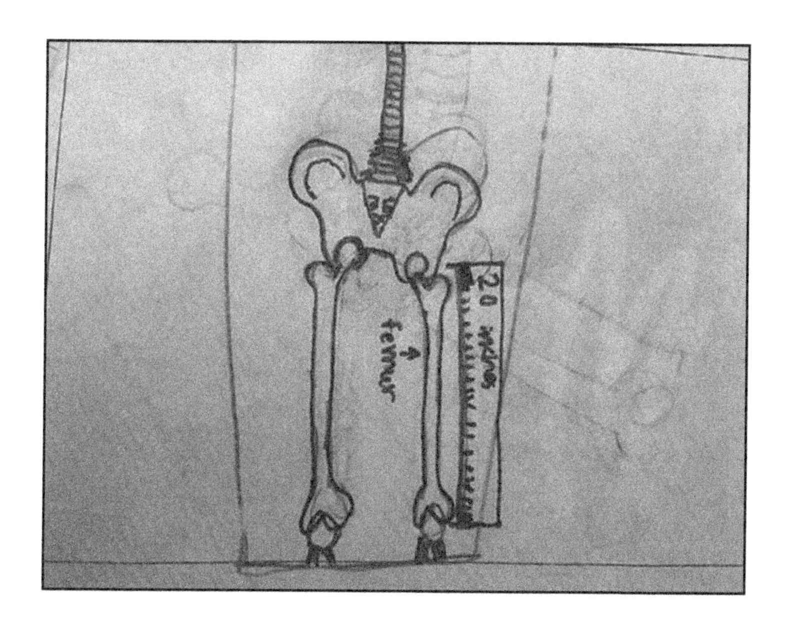
femur
20

THE DANCING PHALANGES BY TAPPING TOE (KAMEERA)

You have three bones connected together they are called phalanges. They are similar to your finger bones. There are twenty-six bones in your foot, and seven tarsal bones in the back of your foot. Your feet help you run, jump, and stand on your tiptoes. Your feet help you balance your weight on the ground. Your feet help you stand sturdy and straight. The metacarpal bone is the second bone in your foot. I really loved learning about the phalanges and all the cool facts.

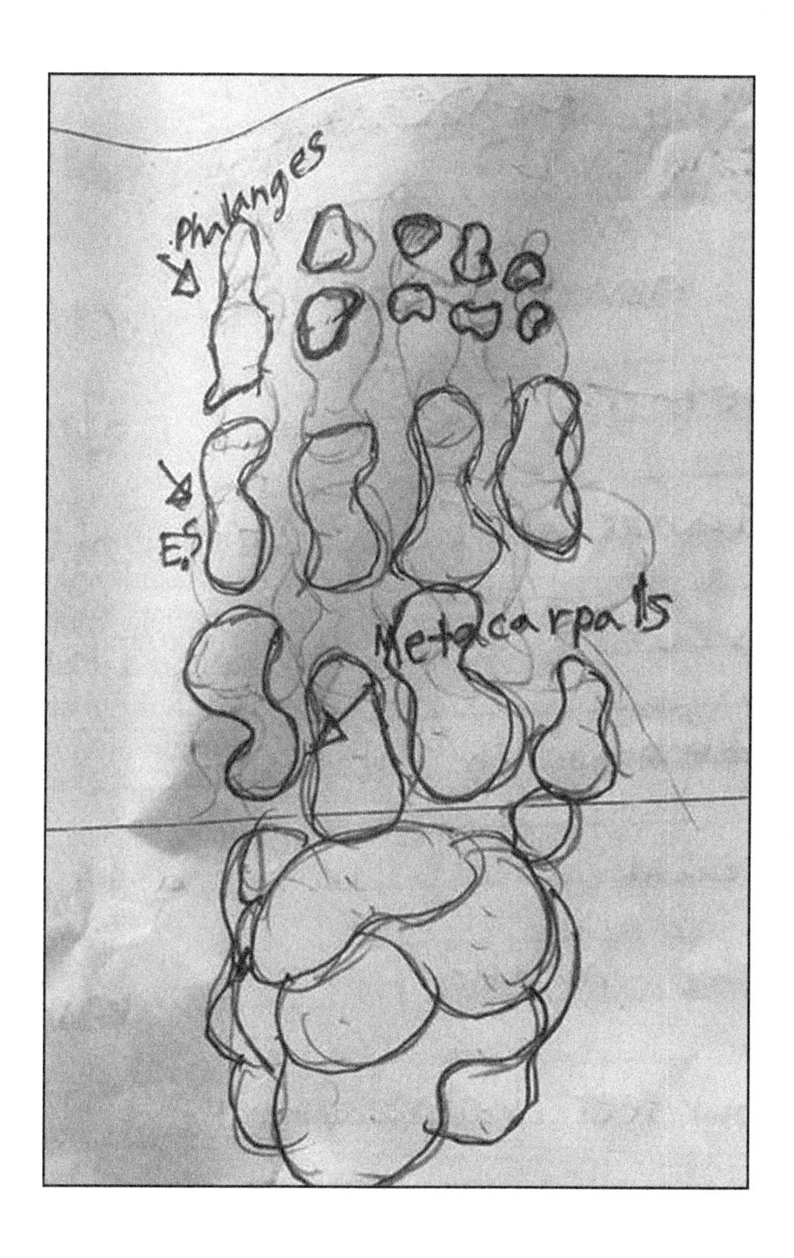
Phlanges
Metacarpals

AMAZING HUMERUS
BY XERNEZ (LILY)

Did you know your upper arm bone (the humerus) reaches from your radius and your ulna to your shoulder (the clavicle)? Your humerus moves with the arm. The bone that connects to your thumb is the radius. The bone that connects to your pinky is the ulna. Your humerus has three names: the humerus, funny bone, and elbow. We learned so much about the arm!

Sources:

Muscles and Bones by Jan Sanderson

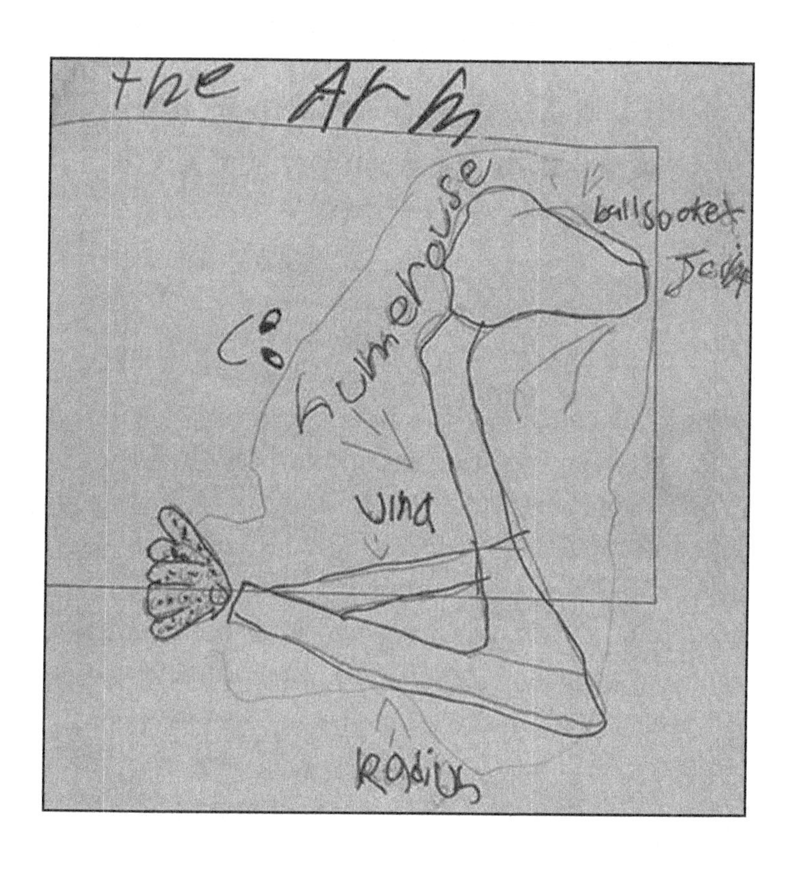
the Arm
humerouse
ballsocket
Ulna
Radius

SMARTS ABOUT THE ULNA AND RADIUS

BY ROSEY (LUCIA)

Did you know the radius and ulna are in between the humerus and carpals, the bones in your wrist? Also your ulna and radius can rotate and move together, letting you twist your wrist and hands? Next your radius is a little bit bigger than your ulna. Lastly, you have two long bones in each arm that are called the ulna and the radius. It was so fun learning about the long arm

Bones!

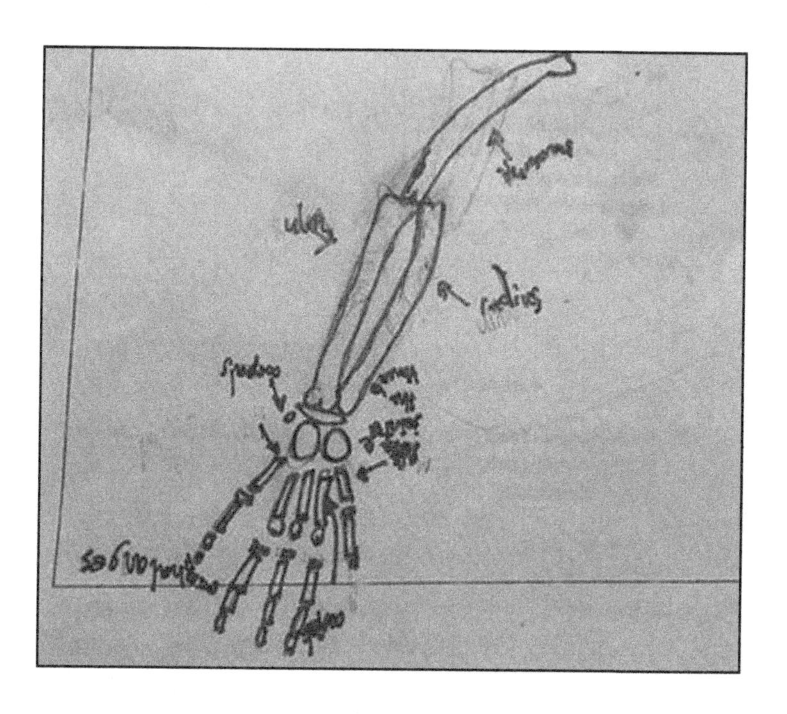

THE TINY FIBULA/BIG SHINBONE BY MILAN (MILAN)

The fibula supports the shinbone, so it can put the patella into place. Without it, you can move all around! You can cause a tibia shaft easily for all ages. Sports injuries and car accidents are easy for tweens and teens. You need both for walking. Without one, you need another! Both are very important.

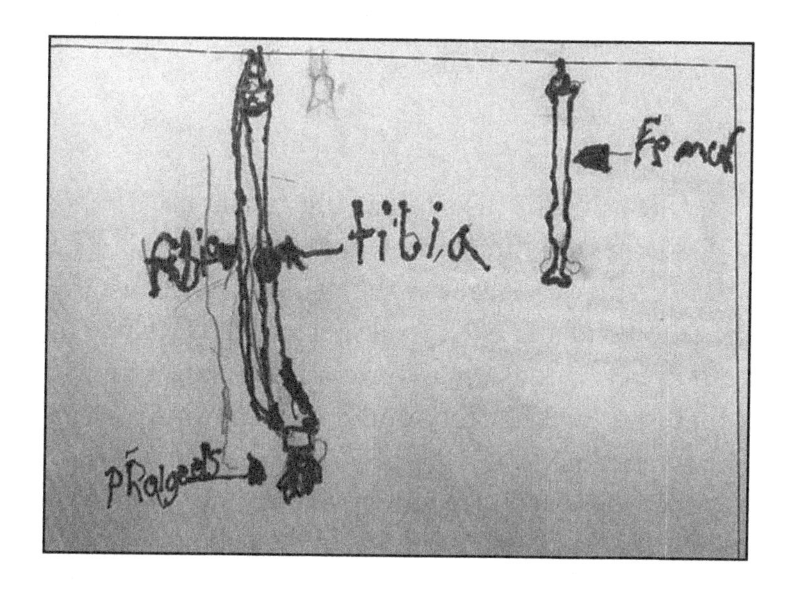
tibia

THE SPINE
BY NATALIE

The spine is also called the backbone. The 33 bones in the spine are called vertebrae. The cartilage between the vertebrae allow the spine to bend and twist. Your neck has 7 vertebrae in your upper back. It has 12 vertebrae. Your sacrum has 5 that fuse together into one bone. And your coccyx has 4 vertebrae.

All of the vertebrae are together because of gliding joints. It's good that we have gliding joints because they help us move our body in different ways.

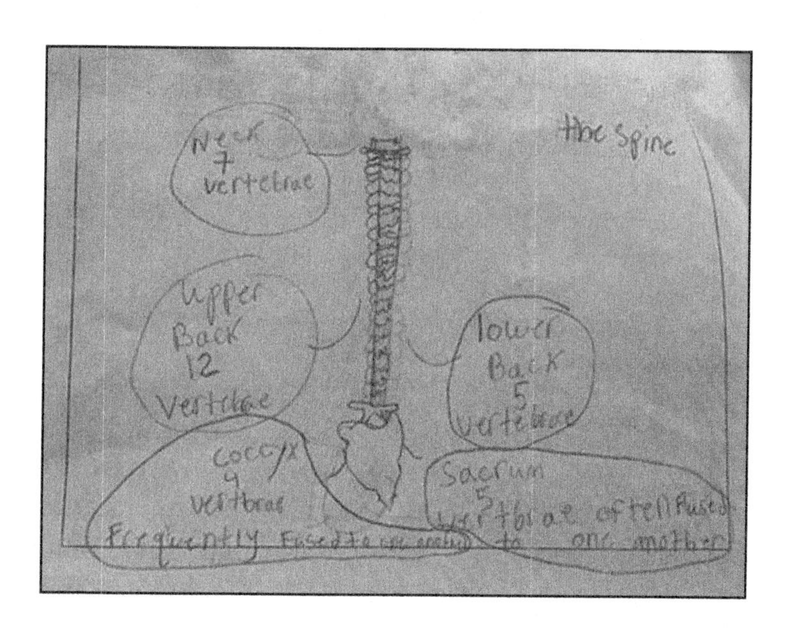
the Spine
Neck
7
Upper
Back
12
lower
Back
5
Coccyx
4
Sacrum
5

ALL ABOUT THE SHOULDER BLADE 24/7 BY DJ (NICK)

The shoulder blade is often called the scapula. The scapula is a ball-socket joint. Also, the scapula is connected to the humerus. Also the humerus is the bone in your arm. The scapula is a ball-socket joint, so it is the most moveable. The muscle around the scapula is called the deltoid muscle. In conclusion, the shoulder blade/scapula is very important to help you move the whole arm.

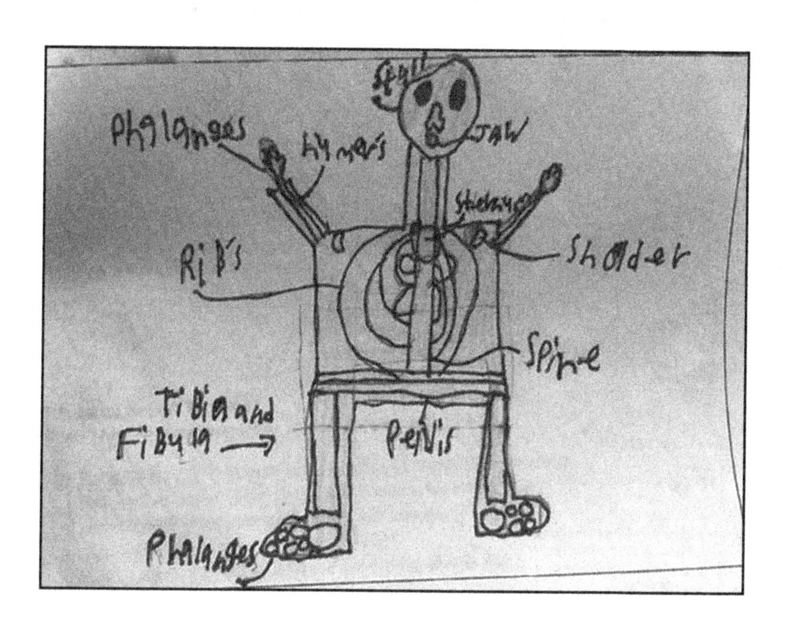
Phalanges
Humer's
JAW
Rib's
Sholder
Spine
Tibia and
Fibula →
Pelvis
Phalanges

THE BONES OF THE BODY
BY PAIGE (PEYTON)

Did you know how many bones there are in your skeleton? Your skeleton has 206 bones. Some other bones are bigger than others. Your skeleton is made up of more than 200 bones. There is just 32 bones in your arm. Nothing can change your skeleton because you have a skeleton inside you.

I am so glad I learned a about the human body.

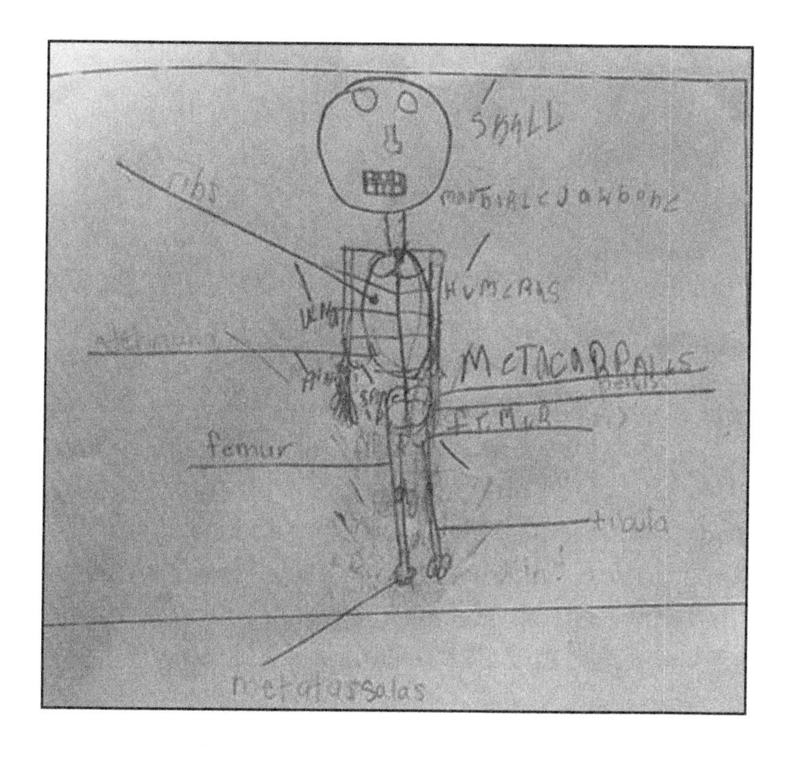
ribs
METACARPALS
femur

THE SKULL OF THE DEAD

BY BLOB (REMIAH)

The skull is made of bone and protects the brain. There are holes in the skull that have nerves and blood vessels. The skull has 22 bones. Only one skull bone can move, which is the jaw bone. Your nose is made up of hard bone and cartilage. The Mexicans decorate a skull mask for Mexico's Day of the Dead Festival. The skull is balanced on top of the backbone. All and all the skull is interesting.

Source:

Movers & Shapers by Dr. Patricia MacNair.

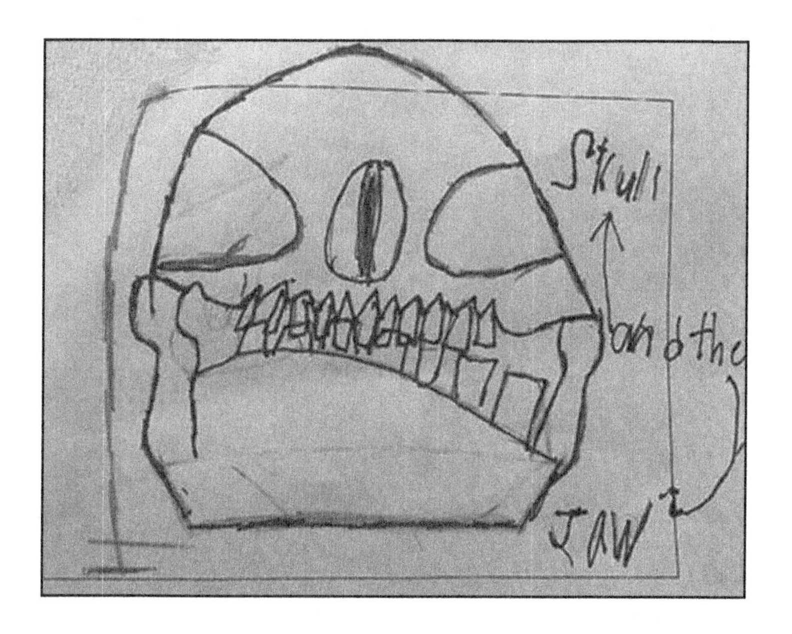
Stkull
and the
JAW

CPSIA information can be obtained
at www.ICGtesting.com
Printed in the USA
BVOW04s1943010617
485808BV00001B/2/P